I Can
Do It!

Baby Mickey and Baby Minnie couldn't wait
for two o'clock to come. That's when they
were going to the county fair. They looked out
the window, imagining all the fun rides.

"See the balloons? I want one!" said Mickey.

"Me, too," Minnie said dreamily.

"Time for the fair! I'll help you put on your coats," called the baby-sitter.

"I can do it!" exclaimed Minnie, putting on her jacket in a jiffy.

"I'll try," said Mickey. He and Minnie sang
the coat song they'd learned at preschool.
    "*Put on your coat, can do, can do!*
    Slip in your arms, not one, but two!
    Up over your head, can do, can do,
    Your coat is on, hooray for you!"

"You already put your coats on!" said the
surprised baby-sitter. Mickey and Minnie were
so proud, they said together, "Can do!"

The Disney Babies climbed into their red
wagon. They were going to pick up Baby
Goofy on the way to the fair.

"Here's Goofy's house!" said Mickey.

Goofy was waiting eagerly for his friends.
"Get your coat on and we'll go," Minnie told him. She couldn't wait to ride a horse on the merry-go-round.

"I put my coat on myself," bragged Mickey.
Goofy said, "Aww, no coat for me. I'm ready
now!" Goofy wanted to go on the train ride.
"Goofy, it's cold outside," warned Mickey.

"Brrr, it sure is!" added Minnie.

"Let's go!" urged Mickey. Goofy started to feel worried. He wanted his coat, but he didn't know how to put it on by himself.

"They'll think I'm a baby if I can't do it," thought Goofy. He looked all over for the arm holes. Where, oh where, did they go?

"There's a hole!" said Goofy, putting an arm through a sleeve of the coat.

"Oops, that's upside-down!" said Minnie.

Goofy tried again. He finally worked one arm
in, but his foot got into a hole, too!

"Help! Let me outta here!" Goofy shouted.
"Here, I'll help," offered Minnie. She gently pulled Goofy's arms out of the backwards coat.
"I know what to do. Remember the coat song, Goofy?" Mickey asked, as he took off his own jacket.

"I can't sing . . ." moaned Goofy.

"Yes, you can," smiled Minnie. "Do just like
Mickey." Goofy set his coat on the floor next to
Mickey's. Minnie sang, *"Slip in your arms . . ."*
Goofy joined in, *"Not one, but two!"*

They all sang out, "*Can do, can do . . .*"
Goofy pulled the coat up and over his head.
"*Your coat is on, hooray for you!*" shouted the
three friends.

"I *can* do it!" Goofy beamed. "I put my coat on by myself!"

"And you sang, too!" laughed Minnie.

The Disney Babies had lots of fun at the fair. Going home, Goofy suddenly yelled, "Help!"

"What's wrong now?" asked Mickey. Goofy answered, "Well, I can put my coat *on*, but, " Mickey and Minnie wondered, "But what?"

Goofy laughed, "I don't know how to take it *off*!" Uh-oh!

Parenting Matters

Dear Parent,

Young children become so excited about every little milestone on their path to independence. With each accomplishment, they joyfully announce, "I can do it!" Learning to do simple tasks, step by step, is an important part of early childhood experiences. Learning to overcome less-than-perfect results and continuing to try until the task is completed is even more important.

In *I Can Do It!* Baby Mickey and Baby Minnie help Baby Goofy learn to put his coat on by himself. Goofy has trouble at first but is then successful, thanks to Mickey's step-by-step example. A special "coat song" from preschool also helps Goofy learn. Goofy feels proud of his accomplishment, and the three friends enjoy a wonderful outing together.

I Can Do It! helps young children learn that:

 * they can complete a difficult task if they break it down into small steps.

 * if they keep trying, they'll get the reward of mastering a new skill and the pride that comes with each accomplishment.

 * accepting assistance from others can help children achieve success.

Some Hints for Parents

 * Encourage your child to learn from mistakes and to see that making an effort is the first step to success, even if the results aren't quite perfect.

 * Remember, tasks that seem simple to adults can be complicated for children. Break down tasks into very simple steps that can be easily imitated.

 * Help your child remember the steps of a task by playful repetition. For example, as you button a button, say: "The ladybug is crawling through the hole. Help her out the other side. Your button is buttoned!"

 * Choose clothing for young children that's easy to put on and simple to fasten.